W9-AGK-168

A Note to Parents and Teachers

Kids can imagine, kids can laugh and kids can learn to read with this exciting new series of first readers. Each book in the Kids Can Read series has been especially written, illustrated and designed for beginning readers. Humorous, easy-to-read stories, appealing characters and engaging illustrations make for books that kids will want to read over and over again.

To make selecting a book easy for kids, parents and teachers, the Kids Can Read series offers three levels based on different reading abilities:

Level 1: Kids Can Start to Read

Short stories, simple sentences, easy vocabulary, lots of repetition and visual clues for kids just beginning to read.

Level 2: Kids Can Read with Help

Longer stories, varied sentences, increased vocabulary, some repetition and visual clues for kids who have some reading skills, but may need a little help.

Level 3: Kids Can Read Alone

Longer, more complex stories and sentences, more challenging vocabulary, language play, minimal repetition and visual clues for kids who are reading by themselves.

With the Kids Can Read series, kids can enter a new and exciting world of reading!

Franklin Has the Hiccups

From an episode of the animated TV series *Franklin*,
produced by Nelvana Limited, Neurones France s.a.r.l. and
Neurones Luxembourg S.A, based on the Franklin books
by Paulette Bourgeois and Brenda Clark.

Story written by Sharon Jennings.

Illustrated by Céleste Gagnon, John Lei, Sasha McIntyre and Laura Vegys.

Based on the TV episode *Franklin Has the Hiccups*, written by Kim Thompson.

Kids Can Read is a registered trademark of Kids Can Press Ltd.

Franklin is a trademark of Kids Can Press Ltd.
The character of Franklin was created by Paulette Bourgeois and Brenda Clark.
Text © 2006 Context*x* Inc.
Illustrations © 2006 Brenda Clark Illustrator Inc.

Kids Can Press acknowledges the financial support of the Government of Ontario,
through the Ontario Media Development Corporation's Ontario Book Initiative; the
Ontario Arts Council; the Canada Council for the Arts; and the Government of
Canada, through the BPIDP, for our publishing activity.

Published in Canada by
Kids Can Press Ltd.
29 Birch Avenue
Toronto, ON M4V 1E2

Published in the U.S. by
Kids Can Press Ltd.
2250 Military Road
Tonawanda, NY 14150

www.kidscanpress.com

Series editor: Tara Walker
Edited by Yvette Ghione
Designed by Céleste Gagnon

Printed and bound in China

The hardcover edition of this book is smyth sewn casebound.
The paperback edition of this book is limp sewn with a drawn-on cover.

CM 06 0 9 8 7 6 5 4 3 2 1
CM PA 06 0 9 8 7 6 5 4 3 2 1

Library and Archives Canada Cataloguing in Publication Data

Jennings, Sharon
    Franklin has the hiccups / Sharon Jennings ; illustrated by John Lei ... [et al.].

(Kids Can read)
The character Franklin was created by Paulette Bourgeois and Brenda Clark.

ISBN-13: 978-1-55337-802-0 (bound).   ISBN-13: 978-1-55337-803-7 (pbk.)
ISBN-10: 1-55337-802-4 (bound).   ISBN-10: 1-55337-803-2 (pbk.)

I. Lei, John II. Bourgeois, Paulette III. Clark, Brenda IV. Title.
V. Series: Kids Can read (Toronto, Ont.)

PS8569.E563F71834 2006   jC813'.54   C2005-900312-X

Kids Can Press is a *Corus*™ Entertainment company

Franklin Has the Hiccups

Kids Can Press

Franklin can tie his shoes.

Franklin can count by twos.

And Franklin can eat his meals

super-duper fast.

Sometimes Franklin eats his meals

a little *too* super-duper fast.

This is a problem.

One day, Bear phoned Franklin.

"Can you come to a movie?" he asked.

"I'll check,"

said Franklin.

He ran to find

his mother.

"Can I go to a movie with Bear?

Please? Can I? Please?" begged Franklin.

"Yes, you may go," said his mother.

"YIPPEE!" shouted Franklin.

"As soon as you eat your lunch,"

said his mother.

Franklin ran back to the phone.

Franklin ate his lunch super-duper fast.

He gobbled up

his sandwich.

He slurped down

his milk.

He swallowed

his cookie in

one big bite.

"All done!"

said Franklin.

He ran to the door.

"Bye!" called Franklin.

And then,

he hiccupped.

Franklin hiccupped all the way

to Bear's house.

He hiccupped all the way

to the movie.

He hiccupped all the way

through the movie.

"SHHH!" said everyone.

"*Hiccup*!" went Franklin.

Franklin hiccupped all the way home.

"Hold your nose and drink

a glass of water," said his father.

Franklin held his nose and drank

a glass of water.

"Hiccup!"

"Breathe into a paper bag,"
said his mother.

Franklin breathed
into a paper bag.

"Hiccup!"

"Don't worry," said his father.

"Your hiccups should stop soon."

But Franklin's hiccups didn't stop.

He hiccupped eating dinner.

He hiccupped in the bathtub.

He hiccupped
in his sleep.

He hiccupped

eating breakfast.

He hiccupped

all the way

to school.

Franklin's friends knew just what to do.

"Hold your breath," said Rabbit.

Franklin held his breath.

"*Hiccup*!"

"Hold your tummy," said Fox.

Franklin held

his tummy.

"Hiccup!"

Beaver sneaked up behind Franklin.

"BOO!" she shouted.

"HICCUP!"

Mr. Owl took Franklin

to the school nurse.

The nurse knew just what to do.

She put a wet cloth on Franklin's head.

She told him to lie on the bed.

She turned off the light.

"Relax," she said.

"*Hiccup!*" went Franklin.

"*Hiccup, hiccup, hiccup!*"

After school, Franklin went to the park.

Jack Rabbit was there.

"Hi – *hiccup* – Jack," said Franklin.

Jack knew just what to do.

"Hang upside down," he said.

Franklin hung upside down.

"Hiccup!"

"Chew gum," said Jack.

Franklin chewed gum.

"Hiccup!"

"Run around the park
ten times," said Jack.
Franklin ran around
the park ten times.
"Hiccup!"

Franklin went home for supper.

"Still hiccupping?" asked his father.

"*Hiccup*!" went Franklin.

"Maybe Granny can help,"

said his mother.

Franklin phoned

Granny.

"Hello?" said Granny.

"*Hiccup*!" went Franklin.

"Hello?" said Granny.

"Who is this?"

"*Hiccup*!"

went Franklin.

Granny hung up

the phone.

Franklin's father

called her back.

Granny came over right away.

She sprinkled black pepper

on her hankie.

She held it under Franklin's nose.

"Take a deep breath," said Granny.

Franklin took a deep breath.

"*ACHOO!*" went Franklin.

"*ACHOO!*

ACHOO!

ACHOO!"

When Franklin stopped sneezing,

everyone waited.

And waited.

"I'm cured!"

shouted Franklin.

Franklin phoned
Bear to tell him
the good news.

"That's great," said Bear.

Then he invited Franklin

to sleep over.

28

"Can I sleep over at Bear's?

Please? Can I? Please?"

begged Franklin.

"Yes, you may go," said his mother.

"YIPPEE!" shouted Franklin.

"As soon as you eat your supper,"

said his mother.

Franklin ate his supper super-duper fast.

He gobbled up his soup.

He slurped down his milk.

He swallowed his muffin in one big bite.

"All done!" said Franklin.

He ran to the door.

"Bye!" called Franklin.

And then …

... he hiccupped.